Hi, I'm Carrie.

An David.

D0901446

Welcome to our **JUMP Up and JOIN In** series.

We hope you enjoy reading the books and joining in with the songs.

This book is called **Elephant's Birthday Bells**.

It's all about **loud** and **soft**. It's lots of fun.

AROO!

Yes, it's very funny. Remember to **turn the page** when you hear this sound . . .

First American Edition 2013
Kane Miller, A Division of EDC Publishing

Text copyright © Carrie and David Grant 2013
Illustrations copyright © Ailie Busby 2013

First published in Great Britain in 2013 by Egmont UK Limited

All rights reserved, including the rights of reproduction in whole or in part in any form.

For information contact:
Kane Miller, A Division of EDC Publishing
P.O. Box 470663
Tulsa, OK 74147-0663
www.kanemiller.com
www.edcpub.com

Library of Congress Control Number: 2012956108

Printed in China
1 2 3 4 5 6 7 8 9 10
ISBN: 978-1-61067-181-1

Please note:
Adult supervision is recommended when scissors are in use.

For our beautiful children
– who teach us all about being LOUD!
– Carrie and David –

For Panda,
the best cake baker ever. x
– Ailie –

Carrie and David Grant

Elephant's Birthday Bells

Illustrations by Ailie Busby

Remember to turn the page when the elephant **aroos!**

Kane Miller
A DIVISION OF EDC PUBLISHING

Elephant's trumpeting
was far too **loud**
for the family band.

And her stomping and stamping was even noisier.

STOMP
STAMP!

So Mom and Dad
went to the music shop.

A few days later it was Elephant's birthday. "What could this jangly present be?" she wondered.

It was some special Birthday Bells!

"The secret to playing them _quietly_ is to be as graceful as you can," Mom said.

Elephant put the bells around her ankles and began to practice.

She *t i p t o e d . . .*

and teetered...

and tottered...

and **tripped!**

But Elephant didn't give up.

She practiced and practiced until she could walk *quietly* on her toes and the bells jingle-jangled beautifully.

She was a quiet and graceful elephant.

The family band
sounded even better
with Elephant's new
jingly-jangly bells.

"I love my Birthday Bells," said Elephant happily.

Play

Chorus:
Ella, ella, ella, Elephant
Ella, ella, ella, Elephant
Ella, ella, ella, Elephant
Play something, play.

Get your bells on.
Not too hard, not too soft.
Get your bells on.
Not too fast, not too slow.
Get your bells on.
Not too loud, not too quiet.
Get your bells on.
Are you ready to go?

Get your bells on.
Not too hard, not too soft.
Get your bells on.
Not too fast, not too slow.
Get your bells on.
Not too loud, not too quiet.
Get your bells on.
Are you ready to go?

Happy Birthday to you!
Happy Birthday to you!

Chorus:
Ella, ella, ella, Elephant
Ella, ella, ella, Elephant
Ella, ella, ella, Elephant
Play something, play something.
Ella, ella, ella, Elephant
Ella, ella, ella, Elephant
Ella, ella, ella, Elephant
Play something, play something, play.

Get your bells on.
Not too big, not too small.
Get your bells on.
Not too high, not too low.
Get your bells on.
Not too sharp, not too flat.
Get your bells on.
Are you ready to go?

Get your bells on.
Not too big, not too small.
Get your bells on.
Not too high, not too low.
Get your bells on.
Not too sharp, not too flat.
Get your bells on.
Are you ready to go?

Happy Birthday to you!
Happy Birthday to you!

Chorus:
Ella, ella, ella, Elephant
Ella, ella, ella, Elephant
Ella, ella, ella, Elephant
Play something, play something.
Ella, ella, ella, Elephant
Ella, ella, ella, Elephant
Ella, ella, ella, Elephant
Play something, play something, play.

Play something, play.
Get your bells on.
Get your bells on.
Play.
Get your bells on.
Play something,
Play something, play.

Happy Birthday to you!
Happy Birthday to you!

When you play Track **7**, the karaoke track, sing along to the whole song! Your special solo parts are in **bold**.

Sing Loud and Proud and Super Soft!

This story was all about **loud** and **soft**.

Learning how to sing or play **loudly** and **softly** is lots of fun.

With your hands on a table (or drum) tap out and count from one to four over and over, like this:

1 2 3 4 1 2 3 4

Now whisper and tap softly.

1 2 3 4 1 2 3 4

Now try it a bit **louder**...

1 2 3 4 1 2 3 4

and now **very loudly**.
(Making sure you don't shout though!)

1 2 3 4 1 2 3 4

If there are two of you, one can call
soft, **medium** and **loud**, and the other
can try to get the commands right.

For our **Jump Up and Join In** series we really want to get children interested in music and how it works. It shouldn't have to be rocket science and we want to encourage you as a parent, teacher or caregiver to teach your children with confidence. If **you** can learn it then **you** can pass it on.

Track 6 **Heavenly Harmonies on the Stairs**

So in this book we're going to be moving on to singing in **harmony**. Look at the picture of the stairs. Let's think about our voice climbing the stairs and counting . . .

1 2 3 4 5 6 7 8

Now one person should sing and stay holding the note on the first step, number **one**.

The other person should count and sing from **one** to **three** and then hold the note on **three**.

Once you've got that you can even try climbing the stairs holding the **odd** numbers up to **seven**, like this:

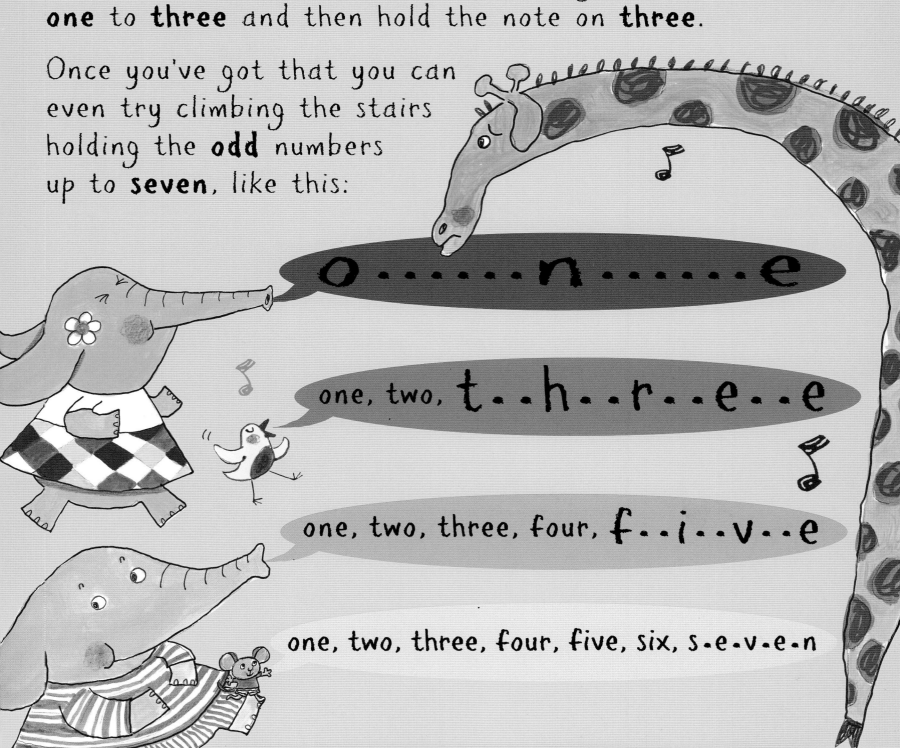

o......n......e

one, two, t..h..r..e..e

one, two, three, four, f...i..v..e

one, two, three, four, five, six, s.e.v.e.n

Make your own
Jingle-Jangle Bells!

You'll need:

Cardboard tube (from inside a toilet paper roll or paper towel roll)
Bells (from old Christmas decorations or your local bead shop)
Pencil   Scissors   Glue   Different colored ribbons
Needle and thick thread

Ask a grown-up to help you!

Step 1 Use your pencil to draw four dots at one end of your cardboard tube. Then repeat until you have gone around the whole roll.

Carefully use your scissors (ask a grown-up to help you) to pierce holes in the cardboard where you have made dots.

Step 2 Use your needle to pull the thread through one of the holes from the inside of the tube. Thread it through your bell and back through the hole in the tube.

Tie the two ends of thread in a tight knot inside the cardboard tube. Repeat step 2 until you have attached all the bells to the cardboard.

Step 4 Now shake those Jingle-Jangle Bells **loudly** and softly, just like Elephant!

Step 3 Glue one end of the ribbon just below the bells and wrap it around the tube. Alternate the ribbons to make a stripy pattern.

About Carrie and David

England's Carrie and David are best known for their hugely successful UK CBeebies series, *Carrie and David's Popshop*. They have coached Take That, The Saturdays and The Spice Girls and have a top-selling vocal coaching book and DVD. In 2008 they were awarded a BASCA for their lifetime services to the music industry.

Parents to four children, Carrie and David are passionate about getting all children to sing and are keen to encourage adults to feel more confident in teaching their little ones music skills from an early age. The *Jump Up and Join In* series was born as a result of this passion and will help young children learn a set of basic skills and develop a real love of music. As ambassadors for Sing Up – a not-for-profit organization providing the complete singing solution for schools in Britain – and judges of the young singers on BBC 1's Comic Relief Does Glee Club, Carrie and David believe children everywhere should be given the tools to enjoy, and to feel confident about, practicing music in all its shapes and forms.

Thanks for jumping up
and joining in!
Till the next time, bye!